George Eliot

Silas Marner

Adapted by Mark Wheeller

T0272729

Salamander Street

PLAYS

First published by Resources4Drama (2014). Originally edited by Clive Hulme.

This edition published in 2020 by Salamander Street Ltd, 272 Bath Street, Glasgow, G2 4JR (info@salamanderstreet.com).

Silas Marner adaptation © Mark Wheeller, 2014.

PB ISBN: 9781913630805
E ISBN: 9781913630799

10 9 8 7 6 5 4 3 2 1

Further copies of this publication can be purchased from
www.salamanderstreet.com

CONTENTS

Acknowledgements

Rachael Wheeller and my family who encourage my commitment to writing these plays. and are always so supportive of my work.

The OYT cast & production team, as listed at the end of the book, for their unbelievable commitment to the project.

Simon Froud & Carley Sefton Wilson for their stream of great ideas throughout the rehearsal period.

Chris Webb Photography.

Charlotte, Froud, Lewis & Natascha who so readily dropped everything to provide me with their memories of this project. Thank you.

Oasis Community Learning and the Principal of Oasis Academy Lord's Hill, Ian Golding, for their incredible support of all things OYT.

Clive Hulme (Resources4Drama) who worked with me to produce the first download version of the play for publication.

George Spender and all in the Salamander Street team for valuing my plays and making the effort to help them extend their reach.

Sophie Gorell Barnes and all at MBA Literary Agents for their on-going support of all my work.

Backgound Note From The Author

In the summer of 2013, I became aware of discussions in the education world led by Michael Gove (then Education Secretary) saying how important it was for young people to be introduced to 'classic' literature. It was this that led me to decide to adapt a 'classic' novel. I always aim to make stories accessible to any audience and hope my version of *Silas Marner* achieves this.

My first thought was to adapt a Charles Dickens story until I remembered a conversation I had with my dad when I was seventeen. At that time, I was on a quest to be the next Andrew Lloyd Webber/Lionel Bart and was looking to write a hit musical. Dad suggested a story he'd enjoyed as a child: *Silas Marner*. I didn't follow the idea up at the time and ended up writing a musical about a sad clown (*Pierrot*) but the little he told me of this story left a lasting impression. I ordered the book in June 2013 and, when it arrived, was delighted to see it was only a short story. I read it and loved it!

By the end of the summer holidays I had completed my adaptation. I treated the book in the same way that I'd used interviews with my subjects when I'm writing a verbatim play. Consequently, almost all the words in the play come from George Eliot's book. I knew this would work as I remembered vividly the wonderful adaptation David Edgar had made of *Nicholas Nickleby* for his incredible *The Life and Adventures of Nicholas Nickleby* which I'd seen back in the early 1980s. It had remained clearly in my memory, particularly how the characters had self-narrated in the third person. This proved to be a further inspiration.

I wanted my Oasis Youth Theatre (OYT) cast to experience the surprise of the plot twists, as they had thrilled me when I had read it, so did not allow them to see the complete script until we came to rehearse each section. Thus, together, they experienced the twists and turns, the highs and the lows. It also served to motivate a real curiosity about what was going to happen. One OYT member cheated and looked up a synopsis online… but she did feel the need to own up, which was sweet!

I decided we should present the play as a promenade performance, which had always been a joy for me. I believe it works best in this format, though I would love to see it performed outside.

My first experience of promenade plays were the National Theatre's

Mystery Plays in the mid 1980s. I have directed four since then, all of them musicals. Many of the cast, who had not experienced promenade before were nervous and sceptical about it. However by the end they were totally convinced. The reviewer loved it! She said:

> *An adaptation of a George Eliot novel might seem something of a departure, but as the play contains only words used in the novel and as Eliot has a great turn of phrase, the production exhibits narrative characteristics of other OYT shows.*
>
> *Writer and director Mark Wheeller has created a beautifully taut and compelling script that he has brought to life with immense skill. Staged as a promenade performance in the slightly smoky space of the transformed auditorium, this was a production of great flair, originality and power.*
>
> *The musical accompaniment, composed by Paul Ibbott, added greatly to the atmosphere and feel of the piece.*
>
> *The youthful cast showed great confidence and command of the material, navigating their way around the space with great panache.*
>
> Karen Robson, *Southern Daily Echo* – for Daily Echo Curtain Call Awards.

Once performed (beautifully) with an incredible puppet playing the pre-teen Eppie, it was taken up by Resources4Drama, a download publisher, and received a few more successful performances as a result.

Where I feel it could be particularly useful is in the English classroom. It would serve to introduce this story to students by way of a pre-organised 'out loud' read, which I always found students loved doing. It reads like a book because it retains the narrative voice of the original. It would give students a perfect overview to the story and an introduction to the style of language used and makes the story more accessible. I'd also suggest you don't allocate roles but literally just read around the class. It will lend itself to that and will make perfect sense. Try it. It saves time on allocating roles and also avoids one or two student having everything to say!

Silas Marner is written to be performed and, when it is, it should be presented with imagination and animation. There are few stage instructions but the ensemble (taking un-allocated lines) can have fun devising their movements. They will create the energy for the performance.

The Principal of Oasis Academy Lord's Hill, Ian Golding, said when I retired from teaching that *Silas Marner* was his favourite of all of the productions he'd seen me put on in the nine years we worked in the same Academy. This was quite an accolade, as it had tough competition including *One Million to STOP THE TRAFFIK*, *Too Much Punch For Judy* (21st anniversary production) and *I Love You, Mum – I Promise I Won't Die* all of which would rate in my opinion as my best ever productions!

I am keen that casts who perform any of my plays avoid standing still when delivering the lines. Enjoy using my adaptation of this story and speaking out loud George Eliot's wonderful words.

Mark Wheeller

You can see Mark talking about the original OYT production of *Silas Marner* on his Mark Wheeller YouTube Channel in his Wheellerplays Series Episode 67.

Photo credits

Charlotte McGuinness-Shaw (Eppie) and Ross Hobby (Silas) with Richard Long's wonderful (Eppie) puppet, at the moment they realise Molly has died from an overdose. The OYT ensemble is in the background.

Emily Moulesdale (Nancy) and James Bratby (Godfrey Cass) are forming their friendship by the beautifully designed tree. You can see the audience in the background giving something of the impression of the promenade aspect.

Both photos by Chris Webb Photography.

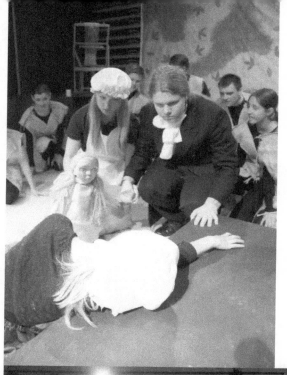

About George Eliot

"George Eliot" was the pseudonym of Mary Anne Evans (1804–1866). Her other works include *Middlemarch*, *The Mill on the Floss* and *Daniel Deronda*. She used a pen-name in order for her work to be taken seriously (female authors were often associated with light, romantic fiction) and to protect her private life. She also wrote poetry.

Characters

SILAS MARNER the weaver of Raveloe
SARAH his fiancée
WILLIAM DANE friend to Silas
DOLLY WINTHROP friend to Silas
AARON WINTHROP her son

MINISTER OF THE CHURCH
DOCTOR
SQUIRE CASS
GODFREY CASS his older son
DUNSTAN *(Dunsey)* CASS his younger son
MOLLY FARREN Godfrey's secret wife
EPPIE their daughter
BRYCE an acquaintance of Dunstan
NANCY LAMMETER Godfrey's true love
MRS KIMBLE Godfrey's Housekeeper

MR SNELL Landlord of the Rainbow Pub
FARRIER a customer of the Rainbow Pub
MACEY a customer of the Rainbow Pub
JEM RODNEY a suspect
JINNY OATES a "witness"
GLAZIER'S WIFE a "witness"

Unallocated Lines

Amongst whom unallocated, non-indented lines are shared at the director's
discretion. The ensemble can also provide the Scoundrels, the Anxieties
and other smaller parts

"A child, more than all other gifts that earth can offer to declining man, brings hope with it, and forward-looking thoughts."

– William Wordsworth

Section 1

SILAS MARNER – BACK STORY

*The unallocated lines (**U L**) should be adopted by members of the ensemble as is appropriate for each individual performing group. The ensemble take on the job of creating the visual setting by playing various props and scenery to set each section. They also help create to the atmosphere of each section by using sound, movement and anything else that may be possible to use inventively.*

The opening lines are there to establish the locale and the ensemble duly make the shape of the community.

ALL: Raveloe…

U L: … a village…

U L: … nestled in a wooded hollow…

U L: … with a fine old church in the heart of it.

U L: … never reached by vibrations of coach-horns…

ALL: … or public opinion.

SILAS: Fifteen years before, Silas Marner came to Raveloe. He worked, weaving linen, in his cottage at the edge of a deserted stone-pit. He sought no man, nor woman.

SCOUNDRELS: Young scoundrels peeped in…

SILAS: Marner fixed on them a gaze…

SCOUNDRELS: And they took to their legs in terror.

U L: Though he was not yet forty, children always called him…

SCOUNDRELS: Old Master Marner.

U L: Nothing in Raveloe had any relation with his old life…

ALL: … his old life…

U L: His old life… in Lantern Yard.

(The cast relocate to establish Lantern Yard.)

U L: In Lantern Yard he was thought of…

ALL: … as an exemplary young man.

U L: And soon became…

SILAS: … engaged to…

SARAH/SILAS: Sarah…

SARAH: … a young servant-woman…

U L: Marner had many friends… one…

WILLIAM: William Dane…

U L: … who was to Silas…

SILAS: … faultless.

U L: A peculiar interest centered on Silas…

ALL: … back in Lantern Yard.

U L: … as once *(**SILAS** holds a sudden still image.)*

U L: … he fell into a…

ALL: … mysterious rigidity…

U L: … lasting over an hour…

U L: … and mistaken for…

ALL: … death.

(Pause.)

U L: There was no medical explanation.

WILLIAM: This looks more like a visitation of Satan.

SILAS: *(Coming out of his rigidity.)* William?

WILLIAM: See you have no accursed thing within your soul.

SILAS: Silas felt pain at his friend's doubts…

U L: Then… *(Someone bursts in to tell the **MINISTER** that church money has been stolen.)*

U L: … after an unexplained robbery…

ALL: … anxiety…

WILLIAM: Silas you are summoned to meet the chapel members.

SILAS: Why?

WILLIAM: You will hear.

U L: Nothing further was said until Silas was in front of the Minister.

MINISTER: *(Takes out a pocket knife.)* This is yours Brother Marner?

SILAS: Why yes. But…

MINISTER: Where did you last have it?

SILAS: I thought it were still in my pocket.

MINISTER: I exhort you not to hide your sin. Confess and repent.

SILAS: What is this? I have done nothing.

MINISTER: You were in the Bureau yesterday, tending our dear departed deacon were you not?

SILAS: I was.

MINISTER: This knife were found in the bureau where there also lain a bag of church money. Some hand removed that bag.

(Pause.)

SILAS: I know nothing about the knife being there, or the money being gone. Search me.

MINISTER: The proof is heavy against you, Brother Marner.

SILAS: Search my dwelling.

MINISTER: No man was there but you.

SILAS: I must have slept, or… or… had another visitation. The thief must have come while I was not in the body. I say again, search me and my dwelling.

MINISTER: Bring in William Dane.

WILLIAM *is brought forward.*

WILLIAM: Brethren. I found the bag tucked behind the chest of drawers in Brother Marner's chamber… empty! *(He shows the bag.)*

SILAS: William? Have you ever known me to lie?

WILLIAM: How do I know what you may do in the secret chambers of your heart to give Satan an advantage over you?

SILAS: I remember now. The knife wasn't in my pocket.

MINISTER: What mean you by these words?

WILLIAM: Silas confess!

SILAS: I shall say nothing more.

MINISTER: Speak out.

SILAS: I have no need. God will clear me.

U L: Resorting to legal measures to ascertain the culprit was against the principles in Lantern Yard.

U L: So, they prayed…

U L: and drew lots.

(They kneel and mumble appropriate Latin prayers.)

SILAS: I must say what sorrow I feel. My trust in man has been cruelly bruised but mine innocence will be certified by divine interference.

WILLIAM: The lots declare…

ALL: Guilty.

MINISTER: You are suspended from church membership. You must render up the stolen money.

SILAS: I do not have this money. God is my witness.

MINISTER: Brother Marner… to confess will be a sign of repentance. Only then may you be received back into the chapel.

   SILAS *turns to* **WILLIAM**.

SILAS: *(Agitated, whispering.)* I never put the knife in my pocket. I took it out last to cut a strap for you William. Why have you woven a plot to lay the sin at my door?

WILLIAM: You speak like a madman Marner.

SILAS: I say you stole the money.

WILLIAM: He is mad!

4

SILAS: God is a God of lies, a God that bears witness against the innocent.

WILLIAM: Brethren, you judge. Is the voice of Satan? We can do nothing but pray for you, Silas.

U L: Marner's trust in God and man was shaken. (**SARAH** *whispers to the* **MINISTER**.)

U L: He took refuge from benumbing unbelief, by working.

U L: Finally, the minister came to him:

MINISTER: I have a message from Sarah.

SILAS: I know what you shall tell me, but tell me all the same.

MINISTER: She holds her engagement to you at an end.

U L: Silas received the message mutely and turned away to work at his loom again.

U L: A month from that time Sarah was…

WILLIAM: Sarah was married to William Dane and Silas Marner departed from Lantern Yard…

… and came to reside in…

(The cast relocate.)

ALL: … Raveloe.

U L: He worked at his loom unremittingly…

U L: … his life reduced to the unquestioning activity of…

U L: … a spinning insect.

U L: His quality weaving had made him a welcome settler to the richer housewives.

U L: By the 15th year of Marner's life in Raveloe…

MALES: The Raveloe men remained wary of him.

U L: Everyone knew he must have laid by a fine sight of money

SILAS: He had taken up bricks under his loom and stored two leather bags there, which held his many coins.

U L: He thought fondly of the guineas…

ALL: … as if unborn children.

Section 2

THE RED HOUSE

U L: Squire Cass's family was the grandest in Raveloe.

U L: His wife had died… some years before.

U L: And… perhaps, this explained why the brothers were turning out so ill.

U L: One November afternoon in their grand Red House…

U L: … Godfrey Cass was with his spiteful, jeering, younger brother,

DUNSEY: Dunstan… known to everyone as…

ALL: Dunsey.

>   (**DUNSEY** *is inebriated.* **GODFREY** *has him by the lapels.*)

GODFREY: Shake yourself sober and listen Dunsey! *(He pushes* **DUNSEY** *away.)*

DUNSEY: Leave me be!

GODFREY: The money I lent you…

DUNSEY: Gave me! *(Laughing.)*

GODFREY: … was Fowler's rent for father!

DUNSEY: You gave it to me!

GODFREY: You promised it would be returned. Father's threatening to go direct to Fowler. Fowler will say he paid me and…

DUNSEY: … and you will get the hundred pounds…

GODFREY: … or tell father I lent it to you.

DUNSEY: Godfrey, you are fortunate I am so good-natured, for if I told father his handsome son had secretly married Molly Farren…

ALL: *(With a sense of scandal in their voices.)* Molly Farren!

MOLLY: *(Cross cutting in, as though in* **GODFREY**'s *dream.)* Godfrey. You have come to see our little baby and me.

6

DUNSEY: Molly Farren – opium addict...

MOLLY: More money Godfrey or else... !

DUNSEY: You would be thrown out of house and home... but... I keep my silence!

GODFREY: Don't flatter yourself your secrecy is worth any price you choose!

MOLLY: *(Cross cutting in as though **GODFREY**'s dream.)* Godfrey Cass if you don't give me money I will make my way to your father and tell him all.

GODFREY: Molly no!

MOLLY: Then money... that's all. Money. You have plenty!

GODFREY: *(To **DUNSEY**.)* She may tell father. I haven't a shilling to stop her... she could be here in no time.

DUNSEY: Then change history, Godfrey. What if Molly took a drop too much opium and made a widower of you?

GODFREY: My patience is pretty near at an end.

DUNSEY: No one would ask questions...

GODFREY: You may urge a man a bit too far...

DUNSEY: I shall say nothing because you are my brother and I know you took this trouble with this loan for me. Think on it.

GODFREY: I might as well tell father everything.

DUNSEY: *(Turning to **GODFREY**.)* I have another idea. Sell Wildfire.

GODFREY: He's the last thing I have. Anyway, I need the money now.

DUNSEY: The Batherley hunt to-morrow?

GODFREY: Batherley?

MOLLY: *(**GODFREY**'s dream **MOLLY**.)* What brings you to my town of Batherley? You have brought me money...

GODFREY: Not Batherley. I can't... and anyway I assured Miss Nancy Lammeter that I would attend the party.

DUNSEY: Then allow me to sell your Wildfire! I shan't look so handsome as you in the saddle, but it's the horse they bid for... not the rider.

GODFREY: I trust Wildfire to you?

DUNSEY: If you don't want to pay father the money, let it alone. I only offer to sell the horse for you.

GODFREY: And you'll sell him all fair and... hand over the money?

DUNSEY: I thought you'd come round.

GODFREY: I have nothing else to trust to.

DUNSEY: I'll get a hundred and twenty for him. *(He exits triumphantly, cracking his whip.)*

GODFREY: Keep sober else you'll... just keep sober Dunsey!

(In the original OYT production the following was presented on a discretely placed screen as a shadow-puppet sequence.)

U L: Dunstan Cass set off on Wildfire in the raw morning.

U L: He passed the stone-pit...

U L: ... and Silas Marner's cottage.

U L: He knew the old fool had a great deal of money hidden there...

U L: How is it he had never thought of suggesting Godfrey frighten the old miser into lending him money?

U L: The resource occurred so easily to him now...

U L: ... and agreeable...

U L: ... that he almost turned Wildfire's head round to suggest the plan to Godfrey.

U L: But...

U L: ... he was much enjoying the self-importance of having a horse to sell...

U L: ... so...

U L: ... Dunsey rode on... and at the Hunt he saw Bryce...

BRYCE: How's that you're on your brother's horse?

DUNSEY: There was an account between us. Wildfire makes it even.

BRYCE: I'll pay a hundred and twenty.

D & B: *(They shake hands.)* Deal.

BRYCE: I'll pay when you deliver to the stables later today.

U L: Dunsey's inclination for a final run was not easy to overcome…

U L: … especially with a horse that would take fences to the admiration of the field.

U L: Dunstan took one fence too many.

U L: Wildfire was pierced with a hedge-stake and…

U L: … unconscious of his price…

U L: … turned on his flank…

U L: … and painfully…

ALL: … panted his last.

*(The shadow puppetry ends as **DUNSEY** falls out of the screen-scene into view. He dusts himself down.)*

DUNSEY: Dunsey reinforced himself with *(hiccup)* a little brandy…

U L: … and much swearing.

U L: He did not mind taking the bad news to Godfrey…

U L: … for he had the idea of…

DUNSEY: Marner's money.

U L: The idea kept growing in vividness…

DUNSEY: Marner's money.

U L: … and the want of it became immediate.

Section 3

SILAS AND HIS PRETTY THINGS...

U L: Meanwhile...

SILAS: Marner had left his house...

U L: ... and treasure...

U L: ... more defenceless than usual.

SILAS: Unpossessing of a jack to suspend his pork while it cooked by the fire, Silas had used his front door key.

SILAS: His mind was at ease as he set off to find twine to set up new work in his loom.

U L: What thief would find his way to the stone-pits on a night as this?

U L: Why this particular night, when he had never come before?

U L: These questions were not distinctly present in Silas's mind...

DUNSEY: As Dunsey arrived in Raveloe he saw light...

*(The person playing the window of **SILAS***'s house pings his fingers out simulating the glimmer of light.)* Light

DUNSEY: ... through Marner's shutters.

U L: The idea of a dialogue with the weaver had become so familiar...

U L: ... that it seemed natural to make his acquaintance forthwith.

U L: The weaver may have a lantern...

DUNSTAN: ... a lantern I could borrow.

ALL: A lantern...

U L: ... a lantern I could borrow...

U L: ... a lantern...

U L: ... a lantern...

DUNSEY: Dunstan knocked...

ALL: … loudly at the door…

(Pause.)

U L: Silence.

(Pause.)

U L: Was the weaver gone to bed?

U L: If so, why the light?

DUNSEY: Dunstan knocked…

ALL: … still more loudly…

DUNSEY: *(Whispered.)*… he pushed the door…

ALL: *(Whispered.)*… it opened.

(Whispered.) Marner was not there.

DUNSEY: *(Whispered.)* Where could he be?

U L: Fetching in fuel?

DUNSEY: *(Increasingly excited.)* Slipped into the stone-pit? If he's dead, who has the right to his money? Who'd know anyone had taken it?

ALL: Where… is… the money?

DUNSEY: Where?

ALL: Where… is… the money?

DUNSEY: *(Laughing.)* Dunsey quite forgot the weaver's death was no certainty.

U L: There were three hiding-places to find a cottager's hoards:

U L: The thatch…

DUNSEY: Thatch. There was no thatch

U L: The bed…

U L: … or a hole in the floor.

DUNSEY: … his eyes travelled eagerly over the floor, where… where there was one spot covered with sand… near the treddles of the loom.

U L: He swept away the sand with his whip…

U L: … found the bricks were loose.

U L: He lifted them up.

DUNSEY: He saw the object of his search.

U L: What could there be but money in these two leathern bags?

U L: No more than five minutes had passed…

ALL: … but… it seemed a long while.

DUNSEY: Marner might be alive. He might return. Dunstan rose to his feet, bags in hand… closed the door behind…

U L: … and stepped forward…

U L: … into the darkness.

SILAS: Marner was no more than a hundred yards away. He reached his door satisfied his errand was done. To his short-sighted eyes everything was as he had left it. Once warm, he thought it pleasant to see his guineas on the table.

U L: Joy is the best of wine.

SILAS: Guineas were a golden wine. He placed his candle on the floor…

U L: … near his loom.

SILAS: He swept away the sand…

U L: … but noticed no change.

ALL: He removed the bricks.

U L: The belief that his gold was gone could not come at once.

SILAS: Have my eyes deceived me?

U L: He held the candle and examined the hole.

U L: He passed his trembling hands all about the hole,

SILAS: Did I put my gold somewhere else and forgotten where?

*(Throughout the next five lines everyone in the ensemble creates the panic in **SILAS'** mind by searching frenetically.)*

U L: He searched every corner.

U L: Turned his bed over…

U L: … shook it…

U L: … kneaded it.

U L: When there was no other place to be searched…

U L: … he kneeled down again and felt once more round the hole.

U L: There was no untried refuge left to shelter from the terrible truth. *(Cast whisper as an echo "The terrible truth".)*

ALL: *(Continue whispering "The terrible truth" under the next few lines.)* The terrible truth.

U L: His gold was not there.

U L: He put his trembling hands to his head.

U L: He gave a cry of desolation.

SILAS: Noooooooo! *(The whispering suddenly stops.)*

U L: The idea of a thief began to present itself.

SILAS: A thief might be caught… and the gold restored!

ALL: His thoughts glanced at neighbours…

U L: … remarks or questions…

U L: … now regarded as grounds for suspicion.

SILAS: Jem Rodney…

U L: … a known poacher…

U L: … disreputable.

SILAS: Jem's the man! He can be found and made to restore my money.

U L: Silas go and proclaim your loss.

SILAS: Squire Cass will make him deliver it up.

U L: Silas ran till want of breath compelled him to slacken his pace to the… Rainbow Pub.

(The Rainbow pub is established.)

SILAS: *(Rushing in. Out of breath.)* Robbed! I've been robbed!

MR SNELL: Master Marner?

SILAS: Jem Rodney. You stole my money…

JEM: Me?

SILAS: Give it me back and I'll let you have a guinea.

JEM: I'll pitch this at you if you…

SNELL: Master Marner, sit down, speak sensible.

FARRIER: The man's run mad.

JEM: Make him sit down.

SNELL: You been robbed?

JEM: What could I ha' done with his money?

SNELL: Hold your tongue, Jem. Hear what he's to say.

U L: Silas told his story…

SNELL: It isn't Jem Rodney as has done this work, Master Marner. He's been a-sitting here drinking his can.

MACEY: Aye, aye. Let's have no accusing o' the innocent, Master Marner.

MARNER: I was wrong Jem. There's nothing to witness against you, only you'd been into my house oftener than anybody else, so you came into my head. I try to think where my guineas can be.

FARRIER: How much money be in these bags, Master Marner?

SILAS: Two hundred and seventy-two pounds, twelve and sixpence, last night when I counted it,

FARRIER: That'd be heavy to carry.

JEM: Some tramp's been in.

MACEY: You two go to the constable's and I'll go with you, Master Marner, to examine your premises. If anybody's got fault to find with that, I'll thank him to stand up and say it out like a man.

U L: Next morning the whole village was excited by the story of the robbery.

U L: The rain had washed away all possibility of distinguishing foot-marks.

14

SNELL: Mr. Snell, the landlord, connected recollections of a pedlar who had called to drink at the house a month before.

ALL: Here surely was a clue to be followed up.

U L: Memory, when impregnated with ascertained facts, is surprisingly fertile:

JINNY: He had a "look with his eye".

GLAZIER'S WIFE: He didn't say anything particular, but it isn't what a man says it's the way he says it.

JINNY: He had a foreign complexion and that boded little honesty.

SNELL: Did he… did he wear earrings?

U L: Everyone who heard the question, with no image of the pedlar <u>without</u> earrings…

ALL: … had one of him <u>with</u> earrings.

U L: And took that for…

ALL: … a vivid recollection.

U L: The glazier's wife…

U L: … whose house was among the cleanest in the village…

U L: … declared:

WIFE: He had big earrings, in the shape of the moon.

JINNY OATES: I saw them too. They made my blood creep.

U L: They make their way to Silas's house.

As they make their way they say the following lines in a cacophonic manner

ALL: I wonder if he called on Silas/Silas will be pleased to hear this /I hope Silas gets his gold back/The pedlar must be the answer.

*(Outside **SILAS**' house.)*

ALL: *(Cacophonic.)* I saw the pedlar at Silas's door/Yes I did too /He went in… I saw him.

U L: There was some disappointment…

U L: … and indignation…

U L: … when Marner said:

SILAS: I have no recollection of this pedlar than he called at my door. He never entered my house, for I wanted nothing.

U L: However, Silas clutched at the idea of the pedlar being...

U L: ... the culprit.

SILAS: It gave him an image of the gold still there...

U L: Silas stepped out and reached towards the image of the pedlar's box in his mind.

ALL: ... still there in the pedlar's box.

Section 4

TROUBLE AT THE RED HOUSE

GODFREY: Godfrey rose the following day to tell his father the distressing news from the day before…

U L: … not to mention the news about Fowler's one hundred pounds!

GODFREY: Father, there's been a cursed piece of ill-luck with Wildfire.

SQUIRE CASS: What?

GODFREY: He's… he's been staked and killed.

S. C.: Thought you knew better than that.

GODFREY: It was Dunsey Sir.

S.C.: You let Dunsey have Wildfire?

GODFREY: Dunsey took him to the hunt to sell him for me because…

S.C: What?

GODFREY: The truth is sir… Fowler gave me your one hundred pounds last month. I'm very sorry… I am quite to blame… Dunsey bothered me for the money, and I let him have it.

S. C.: *(S.C. clicks his fingers to indicate to **GODFREY** to sit down which he does.)* You let Dunsey have… my money? Fetch him to give account of it.

GODFREY: He isn't back, sir. He took some fool's leap and… and did for Wildfire.

S.C.: Is he hurt?

GODFREY: He is made to hurt others. He will never be hurt.

S.C.: Where is he?

GODFREY: We'll hear soon enough, I'll be bound.

S.C.: Where is Dunstan?

GODFREY: He must have walked off.

S.C.: You're up to something and… and bribing him not to tell.

GODFREY: *(Standing.)* You know I'm not a scoundrel.

S.C.: You're a shilly-shally fellow.

GODFREY: If he'd sold Wildfire like I asked, I would have paid you the money.

S.C.: You hardly know your own mind enough to make both your legs walk one way. This lass… Miss Lammeter? *(**NANCY** enters and takes up a central position.)* She hasn't said downright she won't have you, has she?

NANCY & GODFREY: No.

S.C.: Then ask her or let me make the offer for you, if you haven't the pluck to do it.

GODFREY: Please sir, I must manage this myself.

S.C.: Then manage it!

GODFREY: You won't hurry it on by saying anything.

S.C.: I shall do what I choose, and let you know I'm master and, if you know where Dunstan's sneaking… I daresay you do… tell him to spare himself the journey o' coming back home. He shan't hang on me anymore!

GODFREY: I don't know where he is, sir; if I did, it isn't my place to tell him to keep away.

S.C.: Confound it, sir! Don't stay arguing!

NANCY: What had passed about his proposing to Nancy raised a new alarm for Godfrey.

U L: Words from his father would force him to decline Nancy…

GODFREY: … just when she seemed within reach.

U L: Godfrey fled to his usual expectation…

MOLLIE: … that some favourable turn of fortune would save him from any unpleasant consequences.

U L: Weeks passed.

U L: Dunsey's absence was hardly a subject of remark.

U L: He had before quarreled with his father…

U L: … gone off…

U L: … nobody knew whither…

GODFREY: … only to return six weeks later and take up his old quarters…

ALL: … and swagger as usual.

S.C.: To connect the fact of Dunsey's disappearance with that of the robbery occurring on the same day…

U L: … lay quite away from the track of every one's thought…

ALL: … even Godfrey's.

SILAS: Silas sat in his loneliness…

U L: … elbows on his knees…

U L: … clasping his head with his hands…

SILAS: … and moaned very low…

U L: … not as one who seeks to be heard.

U L: The repulsion Marner had always created in his neighbours was partly dissipated by this misfortune.

U L: He was generally spoken of as a…

ALL: Poor mushed creature.

U L: Notwithstanding this…

U L: … Silas spent his Christmas-day in loneliness…

SILAS: … eating his meat in sadness of heart…

GODFREY: No one in Raveloe knew the Silas Marner who tenderly loved his fellow…

DANE: *(As an apparition.)* Brethren. I found the bag tucked behind the chest of drawers in brother Silas's chamber… empty!

SILAS: The Silas who trusted in unseen goodness.

Section 5

SQUIRE CASS'S ON NEW YEAR'S EVE

U L: New Year's Eve.

S. C: Squire Cass's family party

Dance.

DUNSTAN: No one mentioned Dunstan.

GODFREY: Godfrey remained half deaf to his companions...

ANXIETY 1/2: ... anxiety.

ANXIETY 1: Dunsey will be home soon.

ANXIETY 2: There will be a great blow-up.

GODFREY: Not before New Year's Day.

ANXIETY 1: How will you bribe his spite to silence?

GODFREY: Something may happen to make things easier. One pleasure for me is close at hand: Nancy is coming.

ANXIETY 1: Suppose your father brings matters to a pass that will oblige you to decline marrying her

ANXIETY 2: ... and to give your reasons?

GODFREY: Hold your tongue! I feel Nancy's hand in mine already.

ANXIETY 1/2: Anxiety went on, refusing to be utterly quieted...

ANXIETY 1: *(Brandishing a gin toddy.)* What if this?

GODFREY: ... even by much drinking.

ANXIETY 2: *(Pointing out **NANCY** as she enters.)* What if that?

GODFREY: Miss Nancy Lammeter looked bewitching when she arrived.

NANCY: Godfrey behaved as if he didn't want to speak to her.
It was plain he had no real love for her...

GODFREY: … nevertheless, she felt an inward flutter when she saw him advancing to her. *(To* **NANCY***.)* One dance with you matters more to me than all other pleasures in the world.

NANCY: If that's true, I don't wish to hear it.

GODFREY: Not if I turned a good fellow, and gave up everything you didn't like?

NANCY: I am glad to see a good change Mr. Godfrey, but it'd be better if no change was wanted.

GODFREY: Do you want me to leave you be?

NANCY: As you like.

GODFREY: Then I'll partake in a dance with you Miss Lammeter.

Dance.

Section 6

RETURNS AND EXCHANGES

MOLLY: Meanwhile, Molly, wife of Godfrey Cass, with slow uncertain steps, walked through the snow-covered Raveloe lanes…

U L: … carrying their child in her arms.

U L: … a premeditated act of vengeance…

MOLLY: She knew of the great party at the Red House…

U L: … on New Year's Eve.

MOLLY: She would mar his pleasure, with her child that had its father's hair…

U L: … and eyes.

U L: The demon opium was working his will.

U L: Cold and weariness, his helpers.

MOLLY: She sank down against a straggling furze bush…

U L: … an easy pillow…

MOLLY: She did not feel the snowy bed was cold and did not heed whether the child would wake and cry for her.

U L: The little one gently slumbered as if it had been rocked in a lace-trimmed cradle.

U L: Complete torpor came at last.

MOLLY: Her fingers lost their tension. Her arms unbent…

U L: … and the little head fell from her… .

U L: The blue eyes opened wide on the cold starlight.

*(At this point in the original **OYT** production a rod puppet was used for **EPPIE** as a toddler with the puppeteer voicing her words. The puppeteer plays her role when she grows up and, at that point, the puppet becomes her doll.)*

EPPIE: Mammy.

ALL: Mammy's ear was deaf…

SILAS: Since he lost his money, Silas often opened his door to look out…

U L: … as if his money might come back…

U L: … or that some news of it might be mysteriously caught by the listening ear…

U L: … or straining eye.

SILAS: Silas looked out…

U L: … not with hope…

U L: … but with yearning and unrest.

SILAS: He put his right hand on the latch of the door to close it…

ALL: …but… was arrested by the invisible wand of catalepsy.

U L: He stood like a graven image…

U L: … with sightless eyes.

U L: His door open…

U L: … powerless to resist good…

U L: … or evil…

EPPIE: The child's eyes were caught by a bright glancing light on the white ground.

U L: It toddled through the snow to catch it.…

U L: … and when it was reached walked into Silas Marner's cottage…

EPPIE: … squatted down on the hearth… spread its tiny hands towards the blaze…

U L: … accustomed to be left for long hours without notice from its mother…

EPPIE: … it was in perfect contentment…

ALL: The warmth had a lulling effect…

EPPIE: … and the little golden head sank down on the old sack…

U L: … blue eyes veiled by their half-transparent lids…

U L: When Marner's sensibility returned…

SILAS: … he continued the action which had been arrested and closed his door.

ALL: Unaware of the chasm in his consciousness.

SILAS: He went inside and to his blurred vision, it seemed…

U L: It seemed…

SILAS: It seemed as if there were gold… gold in front of the hearth.

ALL: Gold!

SILAS: My own gold brought back to me as mysteriously as it was taken!

U L: The heap of gold seemed to glow and get larger beneath his agitated gaze.

SILAS: … *(Stretching towards it)* his fingers encountered soft warm curls. *(Kneeling)* Silas examined the marvel.

ALL: *(Whispered.)* … a sleeping child.

SILAS: Are you my little sister come back in a dream?

U L: His little sister whom he carried in his arms for a year before she died…

SILAS: How did you come in without my knowledge?

EPPIE: Mammy.

> (**MARNER** *picks the child up and it clings round his neck crying.)*

SILAS: There little one. It'll be alright. Why you have come unto me? Your boots are wet… you must have walked in the snow. Let's go to the door… see if anyone's there.

EPPIE: Mammy.

SILAS: Your Mammy is out here?

EPPIE: Mammy.

SILAS: I can see your footprints little one. Where in the world did you come from?

ALL: He followed their tracks to the furze bushes.

EPPIE: *(Stretching out towards the bush.)* Mammy.

SILAS: What's this here little one… what's this?

EPPIE: Mammy.

SILAS: A human body…

U L: A human body…

U L: … her head low in the furze…

ALL: … and half-covered with shaken snow.

(Dance music fades up and the cast dance as though in the party at the Red House into their next positions.)

Section 7

SILAS REPORTS HIS DISCOVERY

SQUIRE CASS: There were two doors at the Red House by which the White Parlour was entered from the hall.

U L: Both were standing open for the sake of air

GODFREY: Godfrey lifted his eyes and encountered…

ALL: His own child.

GODFREY: His own child carried in Silas Marner's arms.

ALL: All eyes were bent on Marner.

SQUIRE CASS: What do you do coming in this way Master Marner?

SILAS: There's a woman… dead… dead in the snow, at the Stone-pits.

GODFREY: Godfrey felt a great throb.

U L: The woman might…

GODFREY: *(Aside.)* … might not be dead.

NANCY: Godfrey, what child is this?

GODFREY: Some poor woman's been found in the snow.

MRS KIMBLE: You'd better leave the child here, then, Master Marner.

SILAS: I'll not let her go, I've a right to keep her. She came to me.

DOLLY: Did you ever hear the like?

EPPIE: Mammy! *(**EPPIE** clings to **SILAS**.)*

GODFREY: I'll go.

SQUIRE CASS: Send someone else.

GODFREY: No… pass me my hat. *(Puts hat on and leaves.)* Godfrey was unconscious of everything but…

DR: *(Now tending to the body of **MOLLY** inside Marner's cottage.)* … the sudden prospect of deliverance *(**DOCTOR** removes her ring.)* from his long bondage.

GODFREY: If she is dead I marry Nancy, be a good fellow, have no secrets and the child… the child shall be taken care of somehow.

ANXIETY 1: But across that vision came anxiety:

ANXIETY 2: She may live, then it's all up with you!

GODFREY: Godfrey knew not how long 'twas before Marner's cottage door opened and the doctor came out.

U L: I must suppress any agitation I feel, whatever the news.

DR: There's nothing to be done. She's dead. Has been for hours, I should say.

GODFREY: What sort of woman is she?

DR: Young, emaciated, long black hair. A vagrant. Quite in rags. Had a wedding-ring. They'll fetch her to the workhouse.

GODFREY: I want to look at her. I saw such a woman yesterday.

U L: He cast one glance at the dead face upon the pillow.

GODFREY: *(To DOCTOR.)* No, this is not the same woman I saw. *(DOCTOR leaves.)*

U L: He would remember that last look at his unhappy, hated wife.

U L: In these days of no active inquiry he was confident there was no danger she'd be recognised.

DUNSTAN: Only Dunsey might betray him…

GODFREY: No! Dunsey will be won to silence!

U L: Silas entered, lulling the child…

SILAS: … perfectly quiet now, but not asleep.

GODFREY: The wide blue eyes looked up at Godfrey's.

EPPIE: There was no sign of recognition.

U L: The blue eyes turned from him…

SILAS: … and fixed on the weaver's face.

GODFREY: You'll take the child to the parish tomorrow?

SILAS: Will they make me?

GODFREY: Would you really like to keep her, an old bachelor like you?

SILAS: It's a lone thing. I'm a lone thing. My money's gone, I don't know where... and this is come from I don't know where.

GODFREY: You're a good man Marner. I will help you to see she is cared for. *(Handing* **MARNER** *money.)* Let me give something to you to find it clothes. I will speak for you. The parish won't quarrel with you for that right.

SILAS: Sir... why... well, I thank you most humbly from... I'd like to call her Eppie... after my little sister who... who passed when she was young.

GODFREY: Eppie is a fine name.

Section 8

EPPIE REAWAKENS MARNER

U L: Unlike the gold which asked that he sit weaving longer…

EPPIE: … Eppie gradually called him away…

SILAS: … reawakened his senses… warming him into joy.

(**EPPIE** *and* **SILAS** *play.*)

EPPIE: As her mind grew into knowledge…

SILAS: … his mind grew into memory.

EPPIE: As her life unfolded…

SILAS: … his soul, long stupefied in a cold narrow prison, unfolded too…

ALL: … into full consciousness.

U L: Eppie, the weaver's child, became an object of interest.

U L: Everywhere he went folk would sit and talk about the child.

U L: "Why, there isn't many lone men 'ud ha' been wishing to take up with a little un like that".

ALL: There was no repulsion around him now…

U L: The little child had come to link him once more with the whole world.

U L: There was love between him…

U L: … and the child…

U L: … that blent them into one.

ALL: Something had come to replace his long lost hoard.

GODFREY: Godfrey watched Eppie with keen, though more hidden interest, than others. He provided for her and told himself when Dunsey's shadow no longer lay across his path, he would further her welfare, without incurring suspicion.

S. C.: Meanwhile he followed desire.

NANCY: And the accomplishment of…

NANCY & GODFREY: *(They come together.)* … his longest-cherished wish.

Section 9

SIXTEEN YEARS ON... THE SHADOW OF DUNSEY

U L: Sixteen years...

(The cast reposition themselves.)

U L: Sixteen years after Marner found new treasure on his hearth we still recognise...

NANCY: Nancy Cass...

U L: Whose beauty has a heightened interest due to her face showing some human experience.

NANCY: Nancy at home, watching those outside making haste all one way. *(A group run past the house and position themselves by an area marked as the stone-pit.)* I hope nobody's hurt... I wish Godfrey would return.

U L: She felt uneasiness.

U L: ... and the presence of a vague fear...

U L: ... like a raven flapping its slow wing across the sunny air.

NANCY: Nancy wished more and more that Godfrey would return.

GODFREY: Godfrey was there... looking not much different from those sixteen years before...

NANCY: ... unseen by Nancy, hurrying towards their home...

GODFREY: ... looking pale... and trembling as he walks in.

NANCY: Godfrey dear, I am so thankful you've come. I began to get...

GODFREY: ... sit down, Nancy. *(She sits.)* I came to hinder anyone telling you this but me. I've had a shock but I care most about the shock it will be to you.

NANCY: Is it father?

GODFREY: It's nobody living.

U L: She laid her hand on his arm...

U L: ... not daring to speak.

U L: He left the touch unnoticed.

GODFREY: Dunstan...

(Flashback – the lines are shared by the ensemble)

*(The group by the stone-pit are gathered round what transpires to be **DUNSEY**'s body hidden by two large rocks.)*

U L: Is that a skull?

U L: Let's move these rocks.

U L: We'll need help.

U L: *(Calling to the others.)* Everyone. Help.

U L: What's going on?

(They lift the stones aside.)

U L: It's a human skeleton.

U L: It must have been here a while.

U L: *(Picking up a watch.)* A watch?

U L: A gentleman's watch.

U L: *(Picking up a whip.)* A gold handled whip!

U L: This fellow must have been very rich.

U L: Who could it be?

ALL: Yes. Who could it be?

The Red House

GODFREY: They've found Dunsey's body... skeleton. They've drained the stone-pit and there he has lain for sixteen years, wedged between two great stones...

NANCY: He drowned himself?

GODFREY: No. He fell in, and Nancy, there is more.

Flashback at the stone-pit.

U L: *(Picking up a leathern bag.)* What's this?

U L: *(Picking up a second leathern bag.)* What's this?

U L: Open them.

Flashback in the pub.

SILAS: *(Running in, pointing and shouting.)* I've been robbed! Jem... Jem Rodney! You stole my money!

The Red House

GODFREY: Dunstan was the man that robbed Silas Marner. There was the money in the pit... all the weaver's money.

(Silence.)

Everything comes to light, Nancy, sooner or later. When God wills it, our secrets are found out and I... I have lived with a secret on my mind, but I can keep it from you no longer. I wouldn't have you know by someone else, nor should you find it out after I'm dead.

NANCY: I dread what you must say Godfrey.

(Their eyes meet.)

GODFREY: I hid something from you when I married you... something I ought to have told you. The woman Marner found dead in the snow, Eppie's mother was my wife. Eppie is my child.

(Pause.)

I ought not to have left the child unowned.

(Silence.)

NANCY: Godfrey, if you had but told me this, we could have done our duty by the child.

GODFREY: I talked to you of adopting Eppie but you said not to ask what you believe to be wrong.

NANCY: I didn't know she was yours...

GODFREY: And now?

NANCY: What of Marner?

GODFREY: He would be glad for her if we were able to take her on and to show him our gratitude we will provide for him to the end of his life.

NANCY: If we'd had her from the first, if you'd taken to her as you ought, she'd have loved me for her mother and you'd have been happier with me: I could better have bore my little baby dying, and our life might have been more like what we used to think it 'ud be.

(NANCY breaks down.)

GODFREY: I couldn't bear to give you up, Nancy. I was led into marrying that wretched woman and I suffered for it. You would never have married me if I'd told you.

NANCY: I can't say what I should have done.

GODFREY: With your pride and your father's, you'd have hated having anything to do with me after the talk there'd have been.

NANCY: I wasn't worth doing wrong for, nothing is in this world.

GODFREY: I'm a worse man than you thought Nancy.

NANCY: The wrong to me is but little. You've been good to me for fifteen years. It's another you did the wrong to. I doubt that can never be made up for.

GODFREY: Then we take Eppie… I won't mind the world knowing.

NANCY: It's your duty. I'll do my part by her, and pray to God Almighty to make her love me.

GODFREY: Oh Nancy! Then we'll go… well go together to Silas Marner's this very night…

(They hug.)

Section 10

SILAS AND EPPIE

U L: The weaver had undergone great excitement from the events of the afternoon.

SILAS: Sitting in his armchair, Silas looked at Eppie.

U L: On the table lay the long-loved gold…

SILAS: If you hadn't been sent to save me, I should've gone to the grave in my misery.

EPPIE: If not for you, they'd've taken me to the workhouse, and there'd've been nobody to love me.

SILAS: The blessing was mine. A sort o' feeling come across me now and then as if you might be changed into the gold. I thought it'd be a curse if it returned. The money was taken from me and you see, it's been kept, till it was wanted for you. It's wonderful… wonderful!

U L: There was a knocking at the door.

EPPIE: Eppie rose and flushed when she saw Mr. and Mrs. Godfrey Cass and made her little rustic curtsy…holding the door wide for them to enter.

NANCY: *(Taking* **EPPIE***'s hand.)* We're disturbing you very late, my dear.

*(***EPPIE** *moves away to stand with* **SILAS** *opposite* **NANCY** *&* **GODFREY***.)*

GODFREY: Marner, it's a comfort to me to see you with your money. One of my family did you wrong and I feel bound to make it up to you.

SILAS: I count it no loss to me. You aren't answerable for it.

GODFREY: Whatever I can do will be nothing but paying a debt, even if I looked no further than the robbery.

SILAS: Sir, I've a deal to thank you for a'ready.

GODFREY: There are other things I shall be beholden to you for, Marner. That money on the table is but little. It won't go far if you'd nobody to keep but yourself. You have two to keep.

SILAS: I'm in no fear o' want. We shall do very well Eppie and me. I don't know what it is to gentlefolks, but it's almost too much, as it's little we want.

GODFREY: You've done a good part by Eppie, Marner, for sixteen years.

NANCY: *(To* **EPPIE***.)* It 'ud be a great comfort to you to see her well provided for, wouldn't it?

GODFREY: … to see her taken care of by those who can leave her well off, and make a lady of her.

SILAS: I don't take your meaning, sir,

GODFREY: My meaning is this, Marner. Mrs. Cass and I have no children to benefit by our good home.

NANCY: We should like somebody in the place of a daughter to us.

GODFREY: To have Eppie. We would treat her in every way as our own child.

SILAS: My Eppie? *(***EPPIE** *puts her arm around* **SILAS***' head and caresses it.)*

NANCY: It 'ud be comfort to you, to see her fortune made, after the trouble of bringing her up so well.

GODFREY: And you should have every reward for that.

NANCY: Eppie will always love you and be grateful to you. She'd come and see you very often…

GODFREY: … and we'd all look to make you comfortable.

(Silence.)

EPPIE: Thank you, ma'am. Thank you, sir. But I can't leave my father.

GODFREY: It's my duty, Marner, to own Eppie as my child and provide for her.

EPPIE: I don't want to be a lady but thank you all the same. *(She curtsies.)*

GODFREY: I have a claim on you, Eppie. Your mother was my wife. I have a natural claim that must stand before every other.

SILAS: Why didn't you say so sixteen years ago before I'd come to love her?

GODFREY: I know Marner. I was wrong.

SILAS: You might as well take the heart out o' my body? God gave her to me because you turned your back upon her. God looks upon her as mine.

GODFREY: I've repented of my conduct.

SILAS: Repentance doesn't alter what's been going on for sixteen years. When a man turns a blessing from his door, it falls to them as take it in. Your coming now and saying "I'm her father" doesn't alter the feelings in us.

GODFREY: Marner! Be reasonable.

SILAS: You'd cut us i' two.

GODFREY: Your affection for Eppie should make you rejoice. Her lot may soon be fixed in a way very different. She may marry some low working-man. I'm sorry to hurt you, but I insist I take care of my own daughter.

SILAS: I'll say no more. Speak to the child. I'll hinder nothing.

NANCY: Nancy heard Silas's words with relief...

GODFREY: ... as did Godfrey...

NANCY & GODFREY: ... our wish is achieved.

EPPIE: Eppie did not come forward and curtsy. She grasped Silas's hand in hers firmly and spoke with cold decision.
I have no father but one. No one shall come between us.

GODFREY: I haven't been what a father should ha' been to you all these years. I will do the utmost for you, for the rest of my life. You'll have the best of mothers in my wife... that'll be a blessing you haven't known.

NANCY: You'll be a treasure to us.

GODFREY: We shall want for nothing when we have a daughter.

NANCY: It will be our wish you show Marner your love and gratitude.

GODFREY: And... we will make him comfortable in every way.

NANCY: We hope you will love us as well.

EPPIE: I'd have no delight i' life any more if I am forced to leave and know my father is at home thinking of me and feeling lone. He'd no one i' the world till I was sent and he'd have nothing when I'm gone.

SILAS: Be sure, Eppie you won't be sorry if you stay among poor folks, when you might ha' had everything o' the best.

EPPIE: I shouldn't know what to think or wish for with fine things I haven't been used to. I like the working-folks and their ways. I'm promised to marry, Aaron Winthrop, *(**AARON** walks to **C.S.**.)* a working-man as'll live with father, and help me take care of him.

GODFREY: Aaron Winthrop?

EPPIE: We should like to be married. He always behave pretty to you, doesn't he, father?

SILAS: Nobody could behave better.

EPPIE: I wasn't brought up to be a lady.

NANCY: Eppie, there's a duty you owe to your lawful father.

GODFREY: I wanted to pass for childless once, Nancy. Now I pass for childless against my wish. It is my punishment. Marner, you were right. When a man's turns away a blessing from his door it falls to somebody else. We will continue to do what we can for Eppie in this life she chooses. I hope it's not too late to find a way of mending a bit here and there.

SILAS: Will you make it known about Eppie being your daughter?

GODFREY: I shall put it in my will. I shouldn't like to leave anything to be found out, like this of Dunsey. *(**NANCY** and **GODFREY** exit.)*

U L: The next morning Silas and Eppie were seated at their breakfast and he said to her:

SILAS: I have no home but this now. I shall never know whether they got at the truth o' the robbery in Lantern Yard. It's dark to me and will be to the last.

EPPIE: Many things remain dark to us Father. You were hard done by. It seems you'll never know the rights of it.

SILAS: I thought I could never love nor trust again. But since you was sent to me I have loved you. Last evening you said to Mr Cass that you would never leave me.
I trust you. I can trust in you till I die Eppie Marner.
I can love… and I can trust again. You taught me that Eppie. After everything that happened in Lantern Yard… you taught me that.

Section 11

THE WEDDING

U L: One time in the year...

U L: ... lilacs and laburnums show their golden and purple wealth...

U L: ... above the lichen-tinted walls...

U L: A time in Raveloe deemed suitable for...

ALL: ... a wedding.

U L: The sunshine fell more warmly than usual the morning Eppie was married.

EPPIE: She walked across the churchyard...

AARON: One hand on Aaron Winthrop's arm...

SILAS: ... and the other clasped the hand of Silas.

EPPIE: You won't be giving me away, father, you'll be taking Aaron to be a son to you.

GODFREY: *(Making his exit.)* Mr. Cass had gone away to Lytherley...

NANCY: ... for special reasons.

ALL: A pity.

U L: People knew Godfrey Cass felt a great interest in the weaver...

DUNSEY: Marner was wronged by one of his own family.

U L: Explaining how Godfrey provided...

U L: ... the wedding-feast at the Rainbow...

U L: As the bridal group approached...

U L: ... a hearty cheer was raised in the Rainbow yard

ALL: We wish you all joy.

GODFREY: The people of Raveloe had ample leisure to talk of Silas Marner's strange history.

U L: They arrived by due degrees at the conclusion:

SILAS: He brought a blessing on himself by acting like a father...

MOLLY: ... to a lone motherless child.

GODFREY: Master Marner...

ALL: Master Marner deserved his luck.

Everyone cheers.

Confetti is thrown.

There is a country dance involving the whole cast and audience.

Cast Memories of the OYT Production

NATASCHA: In 2013 OYT returned from Paris where we'd performed our first "no words" performance, *Jack*, *(a physical Theatre production based on the Jack and the Beanstalk story)* to an international audience of Drama educators at the *IDEA (International Drama in Education Association)* World Conference. How could we ever follow that up?

Silas Marner?

This was something so very different to anything we at OYT had ever explored previously. I was both intrigued and excited to be doing something set in this period although I knew nothing other than it was a novel written in the 1800s.

It grew to be so much more than that, a tale of morals, feelings, judgements, a story of strong realism and more.

FROUD: I was a part of what had been Oaklands Youth Theatre back in 2008, which became Oasis Youth Theatre after Oaklands was taken over the following year.

Silas started in 2013, so I had been out of YT for the whole of that period but I had reached a stage in my life where I was deeply unhappy with my career choices. They seemed right at the time but had developed over the ensuing five years to being wholly wrong.

I had come away from Theatre in pursuit of a career in the tech industry and a paycheck, which, I thought, I could use to buy the happiness and purpose theatre had previously given me. It didn't. It left me hollow and missing a part of myself.

The feelings of "imposter syndrome" built, until a point of not being able to be contained, when I reached out to Mark asking if it would be possible to return to OYT in a supportive role in his next project, which turned out to be something I'd never heard of... *Silas Marner*.

LEWIS: This was my second OYT project and it was nerve-racking. In the first, with the Intermediate OYT, a younger incarnation of OYT, we had all been pretty much the same age (11-14). In this, I soon discovered I was one of the youngest! Me and my best mate, Ross, who ended up playing Silas, simply saw it as a good chance to have a laugh after school! We knew nothing about *Silas Marner*, just that it was about some old bloke (with the most flamboyant clothes known to man) and his gold coins stashed away back in the 19th century.

It wasn't this specific project that interested me. I wanted to be involved in something where I cared for my fellow cast members, and then, I realised the power of how this morphed into caring about the work we produced as a group... and we really, really did!

CHARLOTTE: *Silas Marner* was my first OYT production (I was in Year 9) and was nothing like what I imagined being part of theatre group would be like.

I'd never heard of the story. Honestly, I had to google it! I thought Mark was crazy to adapt an old George Eliot novel into a play for a bunch of teenagers from an inner-city Academy Youth Theatre group, but... what do I know?

NATASCHA: With this project Mark wanted to do things differently and he drip fed us the script as we came to rehearse it. In each rehearsal we were given a new scene to work on in small groups or as a whole group. This gave a breath of fresh air to the rehearsal process and this made each scene non-preemptive.

I remember thinking at the beginning, Silas was more of a troll in his village, but, as each new scene was given to us, I felt the entire cast warmed to him. We learnt he was a man with a big heart, just as audience would when our play was performed.

LEWIS: I remember us being presented with sections of the script and thinking "right what the hell are we going to do with this bit?". From there, we'd work through five or six ideas, often not getting much done! But those five or six ideas would eventually be intertwined with each other to create the final piece. This was an unusual approach as some nights we'd end with no progress whatsoever, but then get a night where things would just "click"!

CHARLOTTE: Mark is probably one of the most laid back, casual directors I will ever meet. "That could work. Let's try it" is, I think, the best way to explain the process of *Silas Marner*.

Every single suggestion is discussed and tried out, whether it be from a chorus member or the protagonist. Quite often, the original idea didn't work, but another suggestion will stem from that suggestion and the process continues with the entire cast having an input.

It's likely that what was suggested by one person won't be the complete answer, but it starts the process off and, as more and more cast members add suggestions, with Mark's guidance, the single idea suddenly transforms into this amazingly clever piece of theatre.

FROUD: Throughout the years of working with Mark, I've realised he only knows one way of directing, and that is simply NOT to direct. Instead he acts as a curator to the ideas in the room, shaping, evolving, destroying, rejecting and embellishing them.

CHARLOTTE: As the rehearsals go on, there are more and more moments of amazingly clever pieces of theatre created until suddenly at the dress rehearsal, we have tweaked and pieced everything together into one amazingly clever play.

Another beauty of working with Mark is that he isn't afraid to change something right at the very last second. I think that is testament to how much faith and belief he has in the (young, inexperienced) actors he works with.

FROUD: After many years of working in the creative industry I believe the only way to work with people is to allow them to own *their* story and empower them to make choices and then help to shape them. This offers lessons on stage that echo into their own lives.

The opportunity for me to return to OYT allowed me to own my story, and be in the position I am in now.

Mark as a director, and as an educator, is more of a guide. He's a curator not a director.

NATASCHA: Mark engaged very talented people to work with OYT, ensuring we had great props, costumes, backdrops, puppetry etc.

LEWIS: An incredibly important thing happened to me during this show. I was initially playing some very distant farm boy, when one of the cast playing the lead villain had to leave the project. (He suddenly got employment which clashed with rehearsals.) Both Mark and Froud said they thought I would fit the role perfectly so, I swapped potato sacks for velvet suits... and that was fine by me!

NATASCHA: *Silas Marner* worked brilliantly performed as a promenade play.

CHARLOTTE: I had never heard of a theatre production where the audience were not seated and I found this a really interesting way of presenting the story.

NATASHA: A magic aspect of theatre is to make many different locations come alive in one space and have the audience believe in all of them. The promenade style allowed the action to flow from one location to another and created a wonderful atmosphere and a freedom of movement within the piece, which worked beautifully to give grace to the words that we were saying.

FROUD: The audience journeyed with us through the space and the promenade staging added to the feel of moving through time with the characters.

Questions of how do we move from one scene, set in a specific time and place, into an utterly different time and space were only possible to answer with our "organic discovery approach".

NATASCHA: One of the most fun rehearsals was with a professional ballroom dancer, learning the waltz as a team and then using this cleverly in the production to change scene and help the audience to see where the focus of attention had moved to.

FROUD: In order to shape the performance, we took our "organic route", exploring the text as we developed the feel of how we should approach it.

There are clear defining moments, often not pivotal to the narrative, that shaped the production. For instance, how do we move from a moment in Silas' cottage, to a busy pub? How do we make the pub just appear in the moment of the last scene? How do we have the cast immerse the audience around the pub and simultaneously change the atmosphere of that moment?

We had the cast cheer, shout, smash pint glasses together and then move the audience, grabbing them by the arm like a drunk needing help to walk? In this instance, we brought them into the moment and solved the problem.

CHARLOTTE: My mum was definitely not keen when I told her about the promenade presentation style: "A play, where I have to walk? Ridiculous!"

I can just hear her in my head now and please know, she merely said it with an overplayed annoyance at not having a seat. Essentially, she didn't want to stand up and watch a play of a really old book. Also, please know, that my Mum would have watched anything I was a part of... ten times over!

LEWIS: I remember people saying
"It was so immersive and everything felt so real"
... and I'd find myself thinking
"Yeah? Imagine how it felt for us!"
At no point did I ever feel...
"I'm on stage acting."
Every cast member had to be immersed in the world we were creating. Without that, it would've been just another ordinary show.
There really was a 360° stage. But of course it's a high risk demand. If you haven't got the courage to pull this style off, it would have felt like a farm with a few kids running about in potato sacks!

CHARLOTTE: In the end, three generations of my family came to see *Silas Marner*, My little eleven-year-old brother all the way up to both sets of grandparents, and they all loved the play. The live music (by Paul Ibbott our talented music teacher) absolutely transformed them into the setting, as if they were watching the events of the play as they would have actually happened as they walked around the little town.

They all came to watch it a second time around so, it turned out that walking and standing for a play wasn't so bad after all!

LEWIS: A lot of people were overwhelmed by the style rather than the story. It was something they'd never experienced and they said the execution was "genius". The fact that it was a promenade play made *Silas Marner* something very special!

CHARLOTTE: I look back on this production with great fondness. It gave me the confidence to become involved with other theatre projects and enabled me to meet amazingly talented people. Being a part of it gave me a whole new outlook and showed me theatre didn't have to be conventional and the audience don't have to be seated out in-front of you. Theatre can be anything you want it to be.

Where are they now?

Natascha performed in many other OYT productions (I believe she is one of the longest serving OYT members in history!) and features in many of their DVDs including playing Fiona (beautifully) in **I Love You, Mum – I Promise I Won't Die**. She went on to be a Rep for Tui until the lockdown put paid to that in 2020.

Froud went on to study Theatre at the University of Chichester finishing with one of the highest first class degrees. As of 2020, he is an award-winning artist and performer, whose practice ranges from solo performance work, visual art, digital art direction and sound design, and creating experimental technologies in performance. Awards include the IBT (InBetween Time) 2017 award and being a part of the OFFIE 2018 winning Video Design team for Bryony Kimmings 'I'm a Phoenix, B***h', led by video designer Will Duke.

Re OYT he says:
"The only reason I seem to talk extensively about my successes after OYT is because none of this would have been possible without it. The lessons learnt in those productions during my time there, HAVE echoed into my working life."

Lewis looks back with fondness on OYT.
"I turned a fear into a hobby, a hobby into a love, and a love into a career and it doesn't get better than that! I can say for certain that without OYT I wouldn't be doing what I'm doing now."

Amongst other things, he was Jack in the OYT **I Love You, Mum** production and DVD and also played that role in the StopWatch professional touring production a few years later.

He's worked professionally as an actor for over four years on many different projects from stage, TV, film, mixing with some of the greatest people he says he will ever meet. "I've had lunch with Emilia Clarke... but I'm not supposed to tell you that!"

Charlotte became involved in other award-winning OYT productions, most notably Johnny Carrington's **Twisted Tales** which won awards in Theatre competitions. She adapted and extended that performance for her GCSE Drama performance and was (unsurprisingly) awarded an A*.
She is currently at the University of Southampton, studying Neuroscience.

Silas Marner was first Performed by Oasis Youth Theatre (OYT) in 2014 with the following cast:

CAST LIST

Silas Marner Ross Hobby
Eppie/Ensemble Charlotte McGuinness Shaw
Squire Cass Simon Froud
Lady Cass/Jinny/Ensemble Natascha Thomas
Godfrey Cass/Lantern/Ensemble James Bratby
Dunstan Cass Lewis Evans
Molly Farren/Ensemble Anna Pego
Nancy/Ensemble Emily Moulsdale
William Dane/Snell Alex Taylor
Sarah/Macey/Ensemble Jodie Fisher
Minister/Pedlar/Ensemble Joe Tucker
Dr/Glazier's Wife/Ensemble Karmen Arnold
Aaron/Bryce/Jem/Ensemble Boston Sutton
Farrier/Ensemble Adriana Darczuk
Keeper of Gold/Ensemble Nese Somnez
Anxiety 1 Courtney Chapman
Anxiety 2 Paulina Twardowska

Musicians
Accordion Paul Ibbott
Guitar/Vocal Stuart Goodeve

BACK STAGE TEAM

Director Mark Wheeller
Assistant Director Simon Froud
Original Music & Sound Operation Paul Ibbott
Costumes Kat Chivers
Set & Puppet Design/Construction Richard Long
Puppetry & other creative inputs Carley Sefton Wilson
Set Construction Richard Long, Matt Sturrock and Sam Glass
Lighting Sam Glass
Poster/Programme Design Chris Webb

www.ingramcontent.com/pod-product-compliance
Lightning Source LLC
Jackson TN
JSHW080206141224
75386JS00029B/1070